The Adventures of
Ricky Raccoon

Volume Four

written by

G. Brian Weeks

D1366915

G. Brian Weeks

Illustration credits – methmeth from fiverr

Published in the United States of America
 ISBN-13:978-1720602408
 ISBN-10:1720602409
        1. Juvenile Fiction / Action & Adventure /
          General
        2. Juvenile Fiction / Animals / General
          18.07.05

Contents

G. Brian Weeks

Introduction

Hello everyone, my name is John. I'm sure everyone knows me by now. There have been so many changes to Summerville since Ricky started out to find his missing parents. The blueberry fields are alive again and some of the mines are being worked, but we still need more miners. The queen's lake and the river are flowing with fish once again. The village is thriving once more, and we are starting to get some new travelers. However, the town will never be what it should as long as Lord Vladamire and his evil minions of Darkeyes are wandering around the Never-Ending Forest. Ricky has managed to find Queen Holyfield's daughter and son. The prince and the princess are now back at home with the queen as well as Ricky and Baxter. They are trying to figure out a way to destroy Lord Vladamire and those slimy little creatures that smell so bad.

Well, I am excited to tell you and the entire world about Ricky's next adventure. Unfortunately, this is probably going to be my last story I get to tell. You will see why when I have finished. However, I must say this is the most extraordinary sequence of events that I have heard in my life.

G. Brian Weeks

Chapter 1

The King's Lair

Everyone was sitting around the queen's big banquet table finishing up a delicious dinner, when the princess looked up with a tear in her eye at her mother.

"Mother, what did they do with father's body?" the princess asked.

"Oh, my child, on that evil night when the Darkeyes blew that whistle and your father dropped to the floor dead, I didn't know what to do. I just laid there and cried forever. Finally, Jasper, the king's favorite guard and best friend, came and told me the king's wishes if he would ever die. The king is lying in a glass coffin down in his laboratory. I had only been down there once before he died. If I needed him, I would send Jasper or ring the bell. Now, I know my way down there very well and I visit him frequently," the queen said as she hung her head down.

"I want to see him, mother. I miss him so much," the princess said.

"Yes, can we all go down and pay our respects?" the prince asked.

"Yes, let's go. I'll show you the way," the queen said.

So, the prince, the princess, Ricky, and Baxter started to follow the queen to the back of the castle where there was a door. The queen opens the door to a corridor with five more doors. Two on each side and one at the end of the hallway. The queen opens the first door on the right and walks into the room. The queen reached up the wall and grabbed a torch holder and turned it facing down. She walked out of the room and another door opened in the hallway. She did this to the other three doors, until the door at the end of the hallway was finally opened. This was a very complex procedure to get the end of the hallway door opened. This door led to a spiral staircase. The walls were dark brick and so were the steps and very hard to see. Luckily, the torches were lit so they could slowly find their way down.

"Who keeps the torches lit, Your Majesty?" Ricky asked.

"Jasper and the other guards keep them lit so I can come down anytime I want," the queen replied.

"Do you have to do that with the other doors and the torch holders every time you want to come down here?" Ricky asked.

"Yes," said the queen. "You see all the doors will reset right after this door closes behind us. The king didn't want anyone getting his magic whistles."

The door closed behind them and they walked down the staircase, until they came to a door that was locked. The queen counted the bricks in the wall, up and down, until she came to a special brick. She gave it a push and the brick went inside the wall and the door opened. They walked into a warm glowing candlelit room with tables all around the outside. There, in the middle of the room, was the king lying in a glass coffin. They all walked up and looked down at him just lying there.

"Oh, my God, Daddy, I'm so sorry. We will get those things that did this to you. I promise," the princess said in an angry voice with tears in her eyes.

"He looks really good, like he is just sleeping," the prince said.

"Yes, he does, but he is not breathing and has no heartbeat. I'm sorry but he is dead and this is where he will rest forever," said the queen.

Ricky started to walk around the room and look at the tables. In the corner of the room was a metal pot for building a fire. The tables had all sorts of tools, flasks, chemicals, minerals and gold chunks laying all over the place.

"This is one big laboratory," Ricky said. "No wonder the king had all this security to get in here."

"Yes, indeed, and if anyone would come down here, he had a way out by that door over there. Except that door has no locks or tricks, the king told me. If he had to use that door, it would have to be very quick. I have no idea where it leads," the queen said.

"Well, there is only one way to find out," Ricky said.

Baxter jumped on Ricky's shoulder and whispered in his ear. "Oh, you guys, you guys, I won't spoil the surprise. Behind that door, I've been there before," Baxter said in giggly voice.

They opened the door to a tunnel and they started walking.

"If my coordinates are correct, I think we are under the lake," the prince said.

They soon came to a door and opened it, then they were in the treehouse.

"Wow, now I know why that door was always locked from the inside and father told us to leave it alone," the princess said, as she looked at her brother and grabbed his hand.

"So, that explains how the black box of whistles got here in the first place," Ricky said and looked at Baxter.

"The king just told me he put them here for safe keeping. I didn't know how they got here," the queen said while shaking her head.

Baxter jumped up on the table where the case of whistles was and started to laugh.

"Ha ha, loose lips, sink ships," Baxter said as he was slapping his knee.

Chapter 2

Baxter and Britney

The queen, the prince, the princess, Ricky, and Baxter all climbed down from the treehouse and looked across the lake at Lincoln, the giant dragon, just lying there in the grass snoring away. Ricky reached in his pocket and blew the "D" whistle. Lincoln raised his head, gave a big yawn, and flew over the lake and landed right in front of the queen.

"Oh, my goodness," the queen shouted and jumped back three

feet. "I'm not sure I can ride on that thing. I think I will row the boat over myself."

"Oh, come on mother, it's easy. You just climb up there and nestle yourself between a couple of his scales, then grab another scale and hold on. He won't hurt you, but he does kind of hold you with his scales, so you won't fall. Trust me mother, it's just across the lake," the princess told the queen in a reassuring voice.

The queen nodded and followed the princess up the tail of the dragon and found a nice seat. Lincoln stood up and opened his huge wings and started to flap them.

"Oh my, oh my, oh my," the queen kept repeating in a shortness of breath with her eyes closed, as they flew over the lake and back to the queen's estate. The queen climbed down from dragon and said, "I have had enough excitement for one day. I think I will find a delightful book to read and go to bed."

Baxter nestled himself in Ricky's pouch and fell asleep. Ricky, the prince, and the princess built a fire in the fire-pit next to the lake and started making plans to overtake Lord Valdamire.

"We need to go back to Liverpool and talk to your friend named Zephier. I need to find out what kind of minerals or chemicals that I found in that chest from the miner's cave outside of Hammerfield," Ricky told the princess.

"I agree, Ricky. I also need more lightning chips from Zephier. But first, I need to gather more of the ingredients from the caves tomorrow. I am also very curious as to what those ingredients are that you found," the princess said.

The next day, the princess set off early for the caves with a pick axe in her hands. The prince and

the queen were sitting at the table eating. Ricky walked over to the table and saw Baxter and Britney holding hands and walking around the outside of the table just humming a tune.

"Oh Baxter, I see that you are making it official. You and Britney are finally a couple?" Ricky said in a sinister voice.

"Oh yes, they are in love. It turns out Britney's fainting problem was all because she was nervous around Baxter," the queen said as she smiled and rolled her eyes.

"Oh, Sir Ricky, I cannot lie, she caught my eye. She's the bee's knees. I was picking berries, all sweaty and hairy. Then, there she stood right in front of me for just awhile and I just smiled," Baxter said.

"Let me guess Britney, you fainted?" Ricky asked.

"Yes, I couldn't help myself. I love the way he rhymes everything, and he is just so brave, but I am better now," Britney said.

"Then, what did you do next Baxter?" Ricky asked.

"Without a moment's hesitation I gave her mouse to mouse

resuscitation," Baxter said with a giggly voice.

"Well, I'm happy for both of you," Ricky said.

Ricky grabbed a blueberry muffin from the table. Then, he went to the barn and grabbed a fishing pole. Next, Ricky went to the lake and sat at the water's edge next to Lincoln and fished for a while. He was just buying time waiting for the princess to return. Ricky caught several fish and was cooking them in the fire pit for lunch when the princess came walking back from the mines. She had two bags full of ingredients. Shortly afterwards, they all sat down to a nice meal.

After the princess gobbled her food down, she stood up from the table and looked at Ricky. "Let's get moving, Ricky," expressed Princess Hillary.

G. Brian Weeks

Chapter 3

Ant Can't Be

Ricky and the princess walked over to Lincoln. Next, they jumped on Lincoln and the flight soon landed in the field just outside of Liverpool. They walked the field and the cobblestone streets until they came to a man's house with a sign over the door that read, "Alchemist". They knocked on the door and Zephier opened the door and let them in with a big smile on his face.

"Hello princess, what do you have for me today?" Zephier asked.

"I have more phosphorus and sulfur if you could make me some more lightning chips. Also, my little friend here has found some very extraordinary materials in a cave. His name is Ricky Raccoon. Could you tell us what they are? Are they good for anything?" the princess asked.

Zephier took the minerals from Ricky and looked at them. His eyes opened very wide.

"Where did you get these?" Zephier asked.

"I found them in a cave, in a chest, on the road to

Hammerfield," Ricky told the alchemist.

"Well, I can make you one stick of dynamite with these ingredients. That's what this white salt makes. If you could get more of this, I could make some very impressive explosives. However, they can be very dangerous. What do you need them for?" Zephier asked the princess.

"We think we know who stole my father's crown and his magic crystal. We think it is Lord Vladamire. Do you know who he is?" the princess asked.

"Oh yes, he is the man going around trying to buy up

everyone's estates. Nothing ever good seems to follow that man. Find me some more of this glycerol, I could help you with lots of dynamite. Meanwhile, if you could give me an hour or so, I will have your lightning chips and a lightning stick. It is brand new. It is just a wooden stick with chips of the lightning material on the inside. You just strike it against any sharp rock and you will have an instance torch," Zephier said.

Ricky and the princess walked around town for an hour or so and visited some old friends at the Inn where she was staying before. They returned to Zephier and he had everything ready for them.

The princess and Ricky walked back out of town, back to the field where Lincoln was waiting for them. They jumped on Lincoln and flew over to the entrance of the cave. The princess used her new lightning stick as they walked into the cave where the dead miner was discovered. However, the miner was gone.

"He was here, and he was very dead. He was lying over there next to the chest. Maybe a troll ate him?" Ricky pointed and told the princess.

"Was that big hole in the cave's wall there before? It looks like fresh crushed rocks," the princess asked.

"No, it wasn't," Ricky said.

Suddenly, a giant ant came crawling out of the hole. He was huge and hairy and had a giant sharp pincher mouth. Then another giant ant followed him and then another. The princess gasp and tossed her lightning stick to Ricky. Ricky caught the stick with one hand as his other hand was reaching for a whistle. The princess drew her crossbow and bam, bam, bam, they were all dead. They walked over to the hole in the wall and looked

inside. The place was full of the ingredient they needed.

"I know that ingredient needs other ingredients to make dynamite, however, I'm still a little leery of any type of fire in that cave. We could all go up in a big boom," the princess told Ricky.

"I agree," Ricky said. "I have a plan, Princess Hilary."

Ricky gave the fire stick back to the princess and slowly walked into the hole. He then took the "N" whistle and gave it blow. The night became day and the deep dark hole in the earth became as light as day. Ricky gathered up as much of the ingredient as his pouches would hold. He turned around to leave and standing right in front of the exit into the cave was the giant ant queen, and she was not happy. She started using her giant pincher mouth back and forth, like lightning fast scissors and headed straight for Ricky. Ricky reached in his pouch for the "F" whistle to put this giant ant up in smoke, then he remembered what the princess had said. Ricky backed up further down the hole until he found the "S" whistle and gave it a hard blow. The giant ant queen fell fast asleep and Ricky jumped right over her and ran back into the cave.

Ricky and the princess both decided to throw their only stick of dynamite down the hole. They knew if they were ever going to get more of the ingredient that giant ant queen would have to go. So, the princess lit the dynamite and threw it down the hole as Ricky and the princess ran out of the cave. The explosion was greater than they could even imagine. They felt the whole earth shake. They walked back into the cave and looked in the hole and lots of the ingredients were still on the cave's walls and rocks.

Ricky and the princess jumped on Lincoln and flew back to Liverpool and gave all the materials to Zephier. He was shocked at the idea of giant ants and was grateful they were both still alive.

"This is a very delicate matter in making dynamite," Zephier told them. "Give me a few weeks and I will have your dynamite."

The princess gave Zephier a few chunks of gold. Princess Hillary and Ricky walked back to the field and caught a ride on Lincoln back to the queen's estate.

G. Brian Weeks

Chapter 4

The Fly Over

The princess and Ricky landed on the tall grassy meadow next to the lake on the queen's estate. The grass had grown so high and Ricky knew Lincoln would be getting hungry soon. He told Lincoln to eat the grass, so the walk would be easier from the lake to the castle. Lincoln was more than happy to oblige. Soon, the lawn and the courtyard looked beautifully landscaped once again. You could see the flowers growing around the lake and the castle. The paths that lead to the blueberry fields and diamond mines were also cleared out. The prince and the queen were sitting at the gazebo table, eating some fish that the prince had caught from the lake. Ricky and the princess walked over and sat down and told them about the Zephier and the dynamite. They then began to get a game-plan in motion.

"Have you ever been to Lord Vladamire's estate?" Ricky asked the prince.

"No, I just know the road that leads there," the prince replied.

"Well in the morning, after we eat some blueberry pancakes, I think we should have a look from a bird's eye view. Hum, well a dragon's eye view I should say," Ricky said and started to chuckle.

"I agree," the princess said. "We need to find out exactly where this place is and what we are up against."

"I'm not staying here lying on a couch. I'm going with you and will stay in your pouch. We will get it done just like ba-da-bing, we will return the crown of the king," Baxter boldly exclaimed.

"Ok, Baxter, you can come with us, but we are not landing yet.

We are just going to look around for a while and try to stay out of sight," Ricky said.

The next morning, the prince, the princess, Ricky, and Baxter jumped on the back of Lincoln and flew to where the Y in the road was located.

"Ok, the road to the left leads to Hammerfield, so we should take the road to the right," the prince said.

They followed the road to the right until they couldn't see it any longer. The deep forest trees were too thick. They also couldn't see what was beneath the trees, which would really

help. Soon they could see a castle up ahead. Lincoln flew up higher and began to slow down as they approached the castle. They looked down on the castle. It had a huge moat all around it. It was almost like a lake. It also had a very long draw bridge leading from the woods to the castle. The castle was the biggest they had ever seen before. There were guards in heavy armor, all around the castle. They had long sticks with knives on the end of them and long swords across their backs.

"Well, it looks like there is only one way in and out of that castle," Ricky said. "We may have found an effective use for that dynamite Zephier is making for us."

"Maybe," the princess said. "However, every castle has an alternative escape route. I'm sure there is some underground tunnel somewhere just like our home. Besides, how are we going to blow up the bridge with all of them guards around? First, we must get in the castle, find the crown, escape and then blow up the bridge."

"Oh, just like that little sister," Horacio said to Hilary in a very sarcastic voice.

"Ok let's get back before one of the guards see us," the princess said.

Lincoln was flying them back home when Baxter piped up with a brilliant idea.

"Sir Ricky, remember Miranda the queen of the fairies? She was not very tall and not at all hairy. With her swarming fairies, my nose did they tickle. I bet her fairies could put those guards in a pickle," Baxter said.

"That's a great idea, Baxter. When we get home, we will go see her again. Maybe, she would be willing to help us," Ricky replied.

"Oh yea, I remember that road to Liverpool. I had to walk around the mountain because she wouldn't let me pass through her precious paradise," the princess said in disgust.

The next day Ricky and Baxter headed out for the road to Liverpool. Fortunately, there was no trouble on the way. They finally arrived at the forest clearing where Miranda was standing.

"Hello Ricky, how are things going for you?" Miranda asked.

"Well, not so good. I think I could use your help Miranda. You see, we think we know who stole King Holyfield's crown and where to find him. His name is Lord Vladamire. His castle is not that far away, and I know how your fairies can be so sweet and tickle, but also can be a bit distracting. I would like for you to help us with your fairies to distract the guards when we go in Lord Vladamire's castle to retrieve the crown. I could pay you if you wish, Miranda," Ricky replied.

"Well, my fairies do more than just tickle, Ricky. I can give them fairies dust to do a lot more. For example, they can carry dust and drop them on people to make them sleep, or make them cry, or make them hungry. As far as the money goes, you should already know I don't need money. I just have one requirement. Yes, it's a riddle," Miranda explained.

"Somehow, I saw that coming," Ricky said.

"Ok, Ricky, what has only one eye, but cannot see and if you are not careful, it can make you bleed?" Miranda asked.

"A blind cyclops," Ricky shouted out.

"Ha ha, very clever and funny, however, that is not the right answer," Miranda replied.

Ricky looked around at the beautiful meadow full of flowers and the crystal-clear stream. He went down and sat at the rock as he did the last time he was here. He looked down at the stream and remembered the first riddle Miranda gave him. *Who do you*

only see with their eyes opened?
He looked into the stream to see
his own reflection and knew it
was himself. Now this riddle is a
bit different, but still deals with
eyes and seeing.

Baxter jumped out of Ricky's
pouch and landed on a log. He
looked at Ricky and just
shrugged his shoulders and lifted
his hands in the air and said, "I'm
sorry, Sir Ricky, I do not know,
but in your pouch, there is hole.
Stupid me and just my luck, I
moved a bit and my foot got
stuck."

Ricky looked down at the pouch
and saw a small tear. He thought
of his mother and what a great

seamstress she is. Than he thought about her sewing and how many times she had pricked her fingers with the needles. Then it came to him all of a sudden. The answer is a sewing needle.

Ricky turned to Miranda and shouted out, it is a sewing needle.

"Very nice, Ricky, that is two very tough riddles I have given you and you figured them both out. I would be glad to help you when you are ready for us to bring some distractions for you. Here, I want to give this whistle. It is not as fancy as your whistles, but just as effective.

You just give it a blow and my fairies will soon be swarming around and they will know what to do." Miranda said with a smile.

Ricky thanked Miranda and started heading home.

Chapter 5

The Dark Forest

Ricky and Baxter returned to the queen's estate. They were all sitting around the table in the courtyard.

"Ok everyone, I have good news. Miranda and her fairies will help us when the time comes to distract the guards. I know we are still waiting for Zephier to make the dynamite for us, but I think we should travel the path underneath the forest and see what we are up against. I think we should go to the castle first, get the path cleared before we go in carrying dynamite and lightning chips and blow ourselves up," Ricky said.

"Yes, that is a great idea Ricky. We don't know if there are wolves or how many Darkeyes are hiding in that dark forest, between Hammerfield and Lord Vladamire's castle. First, I would like to go into Summerville and talk with your friend Fletcher. Horacio could use a crossbow and I would like to buy some arrows. I have an idea to put lightning chips on my arrow tips. What do you say little brother?" the princess exclaimed.

"Well, I'm not as good as you are with a bow, but I am ready to fight for my father's crown and kill as many of the Darkeyes as I can," Prince Horacio said and sneered with his scarred face shining in the sunlight.

Baxter poked his head out of Ricky's pouch and said with smile on his face. "Sir Ricky, can we stop by your parent's house? You can relax and sit on their couch. Your mom can sew the hole in your pouch?"

"That's a great idea, Baxter," Ricky said and nodded his head.

They all walked the short road to Summerville and visited Ricky's parents and told them of their plan, while Ricky's mom sewed up his pouch. They then walked into Summerville, where I was sitting on a bench next to the river fishing.

"Hi John, catching any fish?" Ricky asked me.

"Oh yes, I can now sell fresh fish in my store for all those who love to eat fish but don't like to go fishing," I explained.

They walked on into town, where the weaver was busy making clothes and blankets and all sorts of things for the traders who visit. The mill grain was turning, and the bakery had several loaves of freshly baked bread and muffins sitting on the store front tables. The saw mill was buzzing away in the background. The whole town smelt wonderful. Fletcher was standing at his fire-pit hammering away at something. They walked over to Fletcher's, the Blacksmith's store, and saw all sorts of crossbows, arrows, fishing poles, hooks, brooms, cedar chests, shovels, pickaxes, metal plows, and hammers.

"Hello Fletcher, I would like to buy several arrows from you. Could you also tie these little sulfur chips on the arrow with the tip? Is that possible? Oh, I need the sharpest tips you have," the princess said.

"Oh yes, it is possible, but that is a tedious job," Fletcher explained.

"Ok, I understand. I will take the best crossbow you have, all your arrows, and the sharpest tips you have. We will tie them on ourselves. Also, we will need a couple decent size arrow pouches to carry our arrows," the princess explained and laid down a sizable chunk of gold on the table.

"Wow, you guys aren't messing around. Here are your arrows and all the tips I have and my two largest quivers. That's what they call arrow pouches," Fletcher explained and took the gold. "By the way, what are you hunting, wolves?"

"Hum, no Darkeyes," Ricky said. "It's a long story, Fletcher."

"Oh, I know all about them. Your friend John has told the whole town about you. Well, good luck I hope you get every one of those nasty creatures," Fletcher said.

They all said goodbye to the town's folk and walked back to the castle. That night, they sat around and tied arrow tips with lightning chips, until they were all done. Baxter and Britney even helped on the project. They all got a good night sleep. The next morning, they jumped on Lincoln and flew over to Hammerfield. It was a bright sunny day and that's just what they needed to head into that dark forest.

"Ok Lincoln, I will blow my whistle if we get into any trouble. I know you won't be able to land, but you can blow and suck the air in and out of the trees to let as much sunlight into the forest as possible," Ricky said.

Lincoln laid down at the beginning of the forest path and watched them walk into the forest. It wasn't very long, and the forest became deadly quiet. There were no birds chirping or rustle of leaves, no squirrels squiring about the place, just dead silence. Suddenly, it became darker and darker and they could barely see in front of them. They could hear the scratching of bark on the trees, hissing, and a horrible smell filled the air like someone had threw up. The princess struck up her lightning stick and there were Darkeyes everywhere, on every tree jumping back and forth, hissing and drooling. They started coming closer and closer. The prince pulled out his bow and started shooting arrows everywhere. The princess did the same and the forest was lighting up. The Darkeyes began to screech and hid from the light.

Ricky blew the "D" whistle and the forest trees were like they were in a hurricane. There were branches falling everywhere. Suddenly, the big blue sky broke through and they could see Lincoln sucking up air and hundreds of the Darkeyes that were hiding in the trees.

"Wow, that was a close one. Now, we must continue onward," Ricky said.

They continued walking the path and soon they were at the entrance of the big draw bridge. They could see the huge castle, which seemed miles away. Ricky reached in his pocket and grabbed the whistle Miranda had given him, he gave it a blow. The guards all over the outside of the castle started sneezing, they laid down and went to sleep.

"Ok, I think we are ready to roll. We can put the dynamite under the bridge when we get it with no problem. I'm also sure one of the sleeping guards will have a key on him, that is if the castle door is even locked. I think it's time to head home now and tomorrow maybe Zephier will have our boom booms ready," Ricky said with confidence.

They all walked back to Hammerfield, where Lincoln was laying by the path's entrance, he was sound asleep. Ricky blew the whistle and Lincoln opened his eyes.

"Wow, how did you do that Lincoln? That was amazing. How many Darkeyes did you eat?" Ricky inquired.

"I'm not sure, but you already saw me clean out lakes and eat anything I want in them. Well, I can do the same with air. I just blow and then suck up the air and eat anything I want inside. Those Darkeyes were not very good and now I have a stomach ache. Plus, I'm too full and sleepy to fly right now. Could you please give me a little while

to rest before I take you home?"
Lincoln explained.

"Oh, sure Lincoln you did an excellent job, take your time. We will walk around Hammerfield for a while," Ricky said sympathetically.

As they all went into town, the town's people were still talking about the giant sea serpent that was killed in the lake. The Innkeeper even offered to let them stay the night for free if they wished. They all decided that Lincoln could use a good long rest and they all had enough excitement for one day. So, Ricky, Baxter, the prince, and the princess all spent that evening around a big fire in the town's square. They had a great meal and listened to the relaxing sounds of the flutes and lutes from the town's musicians. They all got a good night's sleep and the next morning they headed home.

G. Brian Weeks

Chapter 6

It's Go Time

The next morning, Ricky, Baxter, Prince Horacio, and Princess Hilary all flew home and landed on the queen's estate. The queen was standing in her gazebo and there was a package sitting on the table next to her.

"Ricky, this package just arrived for you a few minutes ago. It is from your friend, Zephier in Liverpool," the queen said.

"Oh, if that is what I think it is, it's go time" Ricky said as he carefully opened the box.

Ricky was right that the box was full of dynamite and a note from Zephier.

"Hi Ricky, I know you were anxious to get the dynamite, so I thought I would send my courier and deliver it to you right away and save you a trip."

They all stood and look down at the box of dynamite and then looked at each other and shook their heads in agreement.

"Let's get this over with and get my father's crown back, to put an end to that evil man who killed my father," the prince said.

They grabbed the box of dynamite and flew back to Hammerfield. They started to walk the now cleared path to Vladamire's castle. They soon arrived, and Ricky blew the fairy whistle. The guards were asleep again. Ricky climbed down to the water and used his "W" whistle to dive down and plant the dynamite on the support beams of the bridge. He climbed back up and they all walked across the bridge to the balcony, just outside the castle door. The prince hooked the wires up to the boom box and hid the box around the corner.

"Just one big push down on this handle and that bridge is history," said the prince.

They all took a deep breath and the princess opened the door of the castle and they walked right in. The evil Lord Vladamire was standing right there in his throne room wearing the King Holyfield's crown.

"Welcome, I've been expecting you. I know why you are here and no, you can't have the crown. You see, I have eyes and ears everywhere. Besides the crown is rightfully mine anyway. Aren't you at least a little curious as to why I took the crown?" Vladamire asked with a smirk

on his face.

"Yes, why did you take my father's crown and kill him?" the princess asked.

"You see, your father and I were in alchemy school together and we were partners working on the magic whistle project. This is when I discovered the magic crystal in this crown that give the whistles their power. Yes, I discovered the sleep whistle and the fire whistle. Do you know how much power you could have with these whistles and this crystal? You see your father didn't care about power, but rather trying to use the crystals to help people. Nobody, not even the headmaster understood the power this crystal could give you. However, everyone knew that whoever owned the crystal, would someday be king of the Never-Ending Forest. When it came time to take our final exam, your father was in the headmaster's office talking to him. We all sat down to take the exam and I slightly glanced over at your father. The headmaster accused me of cheating and I was expelled from the school. My family disowned me, and I was forced out of our town and forced to live in the woods. That is where I met my slimy little friends. You see it only takes a small amount of food and they are forever faithful to you. Your father told the headmaster about the death whistle I had made and that is why I was shunned. It was none of his business," the evil Lord Vladamire shouted at the top of his lungs.

"So where are your slimy little friends now?" Ricky asked.

"You don't really think I would keep those creatures in my house, do you? They live in the woods and with one blow of this whistle they will all come and eat you alive. So, you might as well just go home while you still can," Vladamire shouted.

"No, not without my father's crown," the princess shouted as she drew her bow and aimed it right at the lord's head.

The lord quickly blew the whistle and only three minions came running across the bridge and into the throne room. The prince threw a lightning chip on the ground and the minions ran to the dark corner and would not come out. The prince then ran outside and pushed the boom box and there was a huge explosion. You could feel the whole castle shake as the bridge disappeared into the water.

"You, stupid fool, that is the only way out of this castle, but it won't matter to you because you are not going to leave," Vladamire said as he went to blow another whistle.

Baxter jumped from Ricky's pouch and scurried up the pants and shirt of the lord to grab the whistle. Suddenly, the lord blew the whistle and Baxter fell to the ground dead.

Ricky screamed and bent over his little friend. He picked him up in his arms and pushed his ears to his little chest to check for a heartbeat. There was nothing. Princess Hilary drew her bow and was ready to shoot, when Lord Vladamire shouted "Stop!"

"You may be interested to know that on the back of your father's crown, there is a whistle. It holds the crown together. As I was working on the death whistle, your father was working on a life whistle. So, give it a try, little raccoon. You see, his whistle can only counteract my whistle. I could never find anyone to use it on until now. I remember he said something to me like, 'Only true love could make this whistle work and override my death whistle.' So, you want your little friend back and I want to find out if this whistle really works," Vladamire proclaimed.

Ricky took the whistle from the lord's hands and gave it a soft blow into Baxter's ears. Baxter did not open his eyes, but came back to life and whispered into Ricky's ear.

"Oh, Sir Ricky, I was just asleep without a peep. Blow your whistle and make him sleep."

Ricky stood up and yawned. That was the sign for everyone else to plug their ears. Ricky quickly pulled out the "S" whistle and gave it blow and the lord fell to ground fast asleep. Prince Horacio went over and quickly grabbed his father's crown.

"Ok, let's get out of here," the prince said.

"Not so fast. Let's look around this place first. That guy is going to sleep for a while," Ricky said.

Ricky leaned over Vladamire and searched his pocket for the death whistle and the minion whistle. He took them to throw into the lake later. Ricky reached into Vladamire's other pocket and pulled out a small bag of leftover macaroni and cheese. He threw the leftovers at the three minions still hiding in the corner and said, "follow me".

So, they started to look through the castle and came upon a door that led down to the moat. There was a door that led down to a cave with a pool, but no boat. There were fishing poles and lots of fish swimming around. Ricky picked up a pole and dropped the hook and line on top of the water. The hungry fish raced to the hook, hoping it was a piece of food. The three Darkeyes jumped back and opened their big black eyes as Ricky caught the fish. Their mouths began to water, and they tried to beg Ricky for the fish. Ricky gave them the fish. He then told them that they could catch all the fish they wanted and even give some to Lord Vladamire. However, they should never let him leave this castle. The three Darkeyes understood and grabbed the fishing poles, then started jumping up and down, making some grizzly sounds.

G. Brian Weeks

Chapter 7

The Resurrection

Ricky, Baxter, Prince Horacio, and Princess Hilary left the little dock on the moat and headed back up to the balcony of the castle. This is where Ricky blew the "D" whistle and Lincoln came and picked them up. As they flew away, they looked down at the castle, and the broken burning bridge and felt a big sigh of relief. It would be a long time, if ever, Lord Vladamire would leave his prisonlike castle.

It wasn't too long, and Lincoln landed on the grass next to the lake at the queen's estate. First, Ricky jumped off Lincoln and he grabbed the death and minion whistles out of his pouch and ran straight to the lake. Ricky threw the death and minion whistles into the deepest part of the lake, trusting the whistles would not be found.

Then the queen came running out with joy to see they were all still alive. The prince started walking to his mother with the king's crown raised over his head with both hands.

"We did it mother, we did it!" The prince shouted.

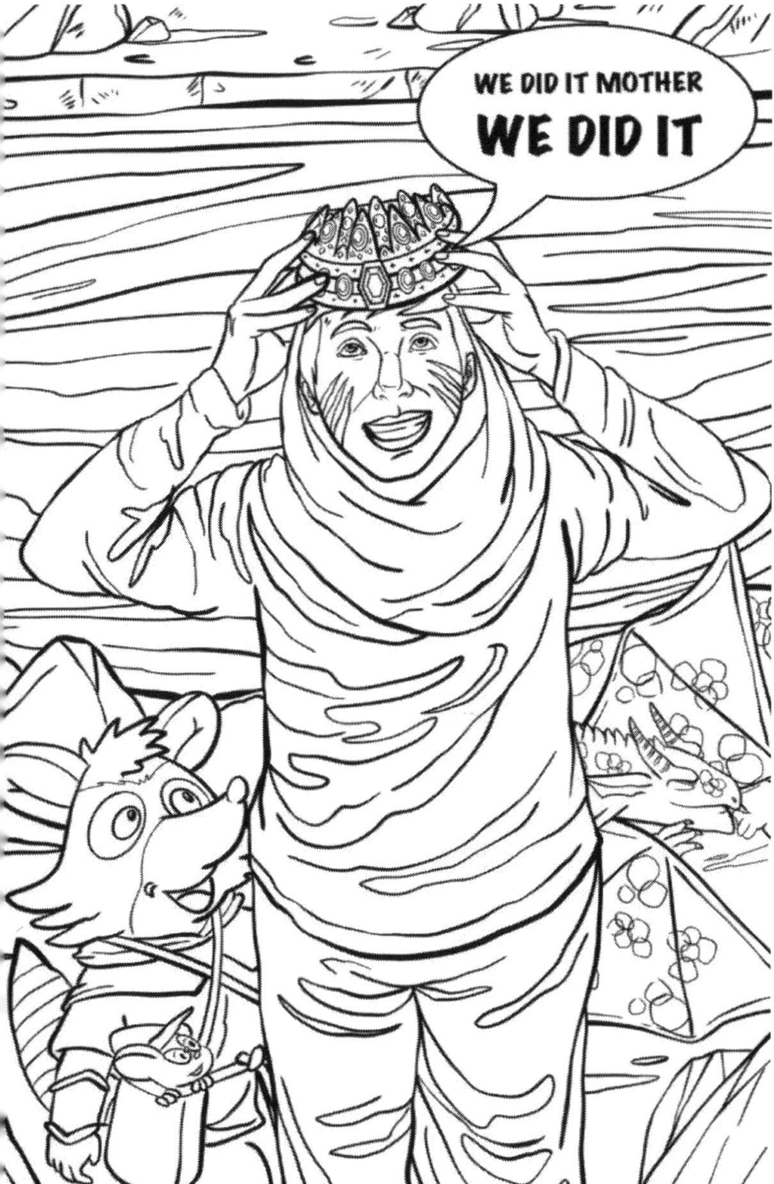
WE DID IT MOTHER
WE DID IT

The queen ran to her son, put her arms around him, and gave him a kiss on his scarred face, with tears rolling down her cheeks.

"You are all very brave," the queen said as she went to hug her daughter.

The princess backed up from her mother and took off her bow, arrows, and her quiver filled with lightning chips. Then she gave her mother a big hug and whispered in her ear. "I won't be needing those things anymore and I'm home to stay mom. I love you so much."

The queen then went over to Ricky and got down on her knees and gave him a hug.

"I don't know what we would have done without you Ricky. I can't thank you enough. You may keep all the whistles I gave you forever as my reward," the queen said, as she took her finger and scratched Baxter's ear as he was poking his head out of Ricky's pouch.

"Oh, Your Majesty, I cannot hide, nor can I lie, but I think for you is a shocking surprise," Baxter said with a grin on his face.

"What are you talking about Baxter?" the queen asked.

"Your husband's crown held another whistle, Your Majesty. I think we should go and visit him right now, if you don't mind," Ricky exclaimed.

The prince and the princess both nodded their heads and started walking toward the castle. The queen looked at Ricky in confusion. Ricky nodded his head and smiled at the queen and followed the siblings to the castle. They all went to the back of the castle and followed the same complex routine until they entered the king's laboratory. The king was still just lying there in his glass coffin. Ricky took out the whistle that was on the crown and handed it to the queen.

"Ok, Your Majesty, lift the lid of the coffin and blow this whistle into your husband's ear," Ricky said sternly as he nodded his head.

"I'm sorry Ricky, but I am scared. He looks so peaceful and the air may decompose his body very quickly. I want to remember him the way he looks now and not a rotting corpse," the queen explained.

"Do you love your husband, Your Majesty?" Ricky asked.

"Yes, of course, I do. I love him with all my heart and I miss him very much, but I can't see what a whistle will do. It won't bring him back," the queen said.

"Trust us mother," the prince and princess both said as they both raised the lid of the coffin.

The queen did as she was told and took the whistle and bent over and blew the whistle in her husband's ear. Then she almost fainted. Everyone else jumped back three feet in amazement, as King Holyfield opened his eyes and slowing sat up.

"Oh, thank you from freeing me from death's prison. I could not move or even take a deep breath. I was very cold and could not shout out for help. I was not in a great deal of pain, just cold darkness all the time. Now, would someone help me out of this coffin. They are for dead people and I am very much alive," the king said as he struggled to get out.

The prince and the princess helped the king out of the coffin and onto his feet. The queen threw her arms around her husband and started to cry and shake in disbelief that he was really alive.

"Are you ok, my dear? How do you feel? What do you need?" the queen asked her husband in a shaky voice.

"I feel fine except I am starving," the king said with a chuckle.

"Of course, let's head upstairs and get you some food right away," the queen said as she grabbed her husband's hand.

They all went upstairs to the big table in the dining room. The servants kept bringing out as much food as they could and as fast as they could. They spent the rest of the evening, telling the king about the fascinating story of Vladamire and the Darkeyes and how they retrieved his crown.

"I knew Vladamire was dangerous, but I underestimated him. I tried to convince him to use his magic for good and not for gold, but he wouldn't listen. I knew someday he would use that whistle, but I didn't think it would be on me. I couldn't stop his plan, even after I told the head master about his death whistle," the king explained as he took a deep breath and looked down at the fire burning in the fireplace.

"You are safe now father, and he won't hurt anyone anymore," the princess said.

"Yes, but just looked at what he did to your brother and all the people in this forest. Look at the damage his wolves and those slimy creatures caused. I should have done something more to stop him," the king said.

"It is over, my dear. We are very lucky this brave little raccoon came along our paths when he did. Without him, who knows the damage Vladamire would have done. He would have ruled the whole forest and those things would be everywhere," the queen said in a consoling voice as she pointed at Ricky.

"Yes, you are right, my dear. Ricky, I owe you my life and will forever be in your debt. Thank you. You may stay here as long as you wish," the king said with a smile on his face.

They all had some blueberry pie and went to bed and got a good night's sleep.

The next morning, they all walked down the road and into Summerville. Everyone was shocked, some people fainted, some people screamed in terror thinking the king was a ghost. The king was really the one who was shocked to see all the improvements of Summerville. The king met Hunter, Axe McCullin, Fletcher and all the new residents of the town. He even came into my store and bought some apples from me to pass out to the kids playing in the town square. It was an unforgettable day.

The next afternoon, Ricky came and saw me at my store in Summerville, and what he told me is going to shock you. You see, Ricky needed some peaceful time away from everything, so he took Lincoln for a long ride high in the sky over the Never-Ending Forest. He could see a blue clearing ahead of him. When he reached it, the forest had ended and there was an ocean or a sea. He flew over it for a while and there was nothing but water and islands. He landed Lincoln on the beach where there were lots of huts. He didn't know if the people were friendly or not, so he kept his hand in his pouch on the "S" whistle. Well, as it turns out, there is a man there named Captain Ron. Apparently, he is having some big problems getting his supplies to the islands because of pirates, headhunters, gorillas and giant snakes. Ricky agreed to help him. So, that is why I told you at the beginning you may not hear from me again. Maybe someone else will share Ricky's next adventure with you.

I regrettably never saw Ricky Raccoon again. However, Summerville continued to thrive and Holyfields were more successful than ever before. Neither will never forget everything Ricky did for them. Oh, yes before I forget, it is rumored that two little mice named Baxter and Britney got married. I think it is true, Baxter has put on a lot of weight lately.

Well, that concludes the first saga of "The Adventures of Ricky Raccoon". It's been my pleasure sharing these adventures with you.

Sincerely,

John

The End

Whistles given to Ricky Raccoon from Queen Holyfield:

The **S** whistle puts everyone around you asleep when you blow it.

The **L** whistle levitates you three feet above the ground when you blow it.

The **N** whistle is for night vision. When you blow it, you can see during the night.

The **F** whistle is for a fiery explosion all around you.

The **H** whistle is for hilarious laughter. When you blow it, everyone around you will start to laugh uncontrollably.

The **C** whistle is for camouflage. When you blow this whistle, you become invisible for just a brief time.

Whistles found by Ricky Raccoon:

The **D** whistle is for dragon. When you blow it, Lincoln the dragon will come to that person for a ride or their needs.

The **W** whistle is for water breathing. Water will become clear like the blue sky, and you can breathe water just like air.